A Little at a Time

by DAVID A. ADLER ◆ illustrated by PAUL TONG

Holiday House / New York

With love, to Renée
    D. A. A.

For Yéye and Leigh
    P. T.

Text copyright © 1976, 2010 by David A. Adler
Illustrations copyright © 2010 by Paul Tong
A Little at a Time was published first by Random House, Inc. in 1976 with illustrations by N. M. Bodecker.
The text for this new edition incorporates minor changes by the author.
All Rights Reserved
HOLIDAY HOUSE is registered in the U.S. Patent and Trademark Office.
Printed and bound in March 2010 at Kwong Fat Offset Co., Ltd., Dongguan City,
Quang Dong Province, China.
The text typeface is Breughel.
The artwork was created with oil paint on Fabriano watercolor paper.
www.holidayhouse.com
1 3 5 7 9 10 8 6 4 2

Library of Congress Cataloging-in-Publication Data
Adler, David A.
A little at a time / by David A. Adler ; illustrated by Paul Tong. — 1st ed.
p. cm.
Summary: While enjoying a morning together, a little boy asks his grandfather a series of questions
about how things got to be the way they are, such as tall trees, deep holes, and big dinosaurs in the museum
they visit, but Grandpa's answer is always the same.
ISBN 978-0-8234-1739-1 (hardcover)
[1. Questions and answers—Fiction. 2. Grandfathers—Fiction.] I. Tong, Paul, ill. II. Title.
PZ7.A2615Aaf 2010
[E]—dc22
2009008166

How did that tree get
to be so tall, Grandpa?
How did it get so tall?

When it started
it was just a seed.
Then it grew
and grew and grew,
but it only grew
a little at a time.

And how come I'm so small?

When I was your age
I was smaller than you.
You'll grow,
not as tall as that tree
but maybe taller than me.
You'll grow
the way I grew,
a little at a time.

How did this hole get to be so deep?
How did it get so deep?

Watch that big shovel.
Each time the shovel drops down
and digs up some dirt,
the hole gets deeper.

But, Grandpa,
the hole doesn't look any deeper.

But it is!
It's just hard to notice
when something changes
a little at a time.

Were the buildings here always this high, Grandpa?

Buildings here were much smaller
when I was your age.
But as more room was needed,
small buildings were torn down
and on the same land
higher buildings were built.
A city this big
is always changing
a little at a time.

Grandpa, why is this street so dirty?
How did it get like this?

Many people drop things.
Each person may drop
only a little,
but with so many people
dropping just a little,
this street became dirty
a little at a time.

And the air, Grandpa,
it's so full of smoke.
Why?

Cars, buses, trucks, chimneys—
all give off smoke.
And with so many things
giving off a little smoke,
the air became dirty
the same as the street—
a little at a time.

Look at all these steps, Grandpa.
Watch how fast I get to the top!

If you race to the top
you'll leave me behind,
and you'll be too tired
to see the museum.
Climb the way I climb,
a little at a time.

What are we going to see, Grandpa?

We'll see some moon rocks
and some meteorites,
and of course the dinosaurs.

But what about the white whales?

We'll see the whales
on another day.
A museum this big
can only be seen
a little at a time.

Wow, Grandpa!
What is this?

This is a skeleton of a large
dinosaur,
the *Tyrannosaurus rex*.

It sure is big, Grandpa.

Yes, it is big;
and it took a long time
to put it together.
Scientists dug up the bones
and cleaned them.
Then they had to learn
where each bone belonged.
It was hard work,
just like doing a puzzle.

I know how they did it, Grandpa—
a little at a time.

Come on, Grandpa.
I'm almost finished.
Why do you eat so slow?

You like ice cream,
so you eat it quickly.
I like ice cream too.
But to me it tastes better
and lasts so much longer
if I eat it
a little at a time.

It's time now
to start going home,
but don't run ahead.
Your grandpa travels just
a little at a time.

How did you get to be so smart,
Grandpa?
How did you learn so much?

I'm just like you.
I ask many questions,
and little by little
I learn a lot.
As long as I keep asking,
I'll keep learning
a little at a time.

I think it's time for your afternoon nap.

But how did it get so late, Grandpa?

You should know
the answer to that.
The morning is over
very quickly, it seems,
but really it went by
just like everything else—
a little at a time.